MAUBY'S QUEST
for the
Magic Flower

By PETER LAURIE
Illustrated by H. ANN DODSON

For Christopher and Pam

MACMILLAN
CARIBBEAN

Mauby the cat was having a nap.

She was dreaming that she was lying beside a gurgling stream. The stream was full of delicious warm milk. Little fat fish from time to time would leap out of the stream and land in her open mouth.

Suddenly a slimy green eel leaped out of the stream and flopped onto her belly. Mauby gave a loud screech. She woke up to find Bongo, the farm dog, panting over her with his long red tongue.

'What are you doing? Go away, you filthy dog!' Mauby was not too fond of Bongo. He barked at her and chased her. Besides he had the nasty habit of playing with dead frogs and smelt terrible.

Wake up, Mauby!' said Bongo, 'You've got to help us.'

Mauby saw that Tiki-Tak, the blackbird, was perched on the water trough and Myra, the cow, was standing next to Bongo. Mauby did not trust either of them. Tiki-Tak had almost pecked off her ear for chasing one of her little ones and Myra had butted her for trying to catch an egret that was picking ticks off her back. They all lived on a small farm in the foothills of a sunny green island in the Caribbean Sea.

'Help you?' said Mauby. 'Since when have you wanted *me* to help you?'

'Well,' said Myra in her slow, deep voice, 'my young calf is very sick and Farmer Hunte and the vet don't know what's wrong, so they can't cure her. She has eaten a poisonous weed and there is only one thing that can make her better. That's the flower of a vine that grows only in a cave up in the mountains. If she doesn't get that soon, she'll die. So we hoped you'd go and get the flower for us.'

'You must be mad if you think I'm leaving this farm again,' snorted Mauby. 'The last time I left, I nearly got run over by a truck, swallowed by an enormous snake, eaten by a shark and drowned in the sea. No way am I setting foot outside this yard again.' And, flicking her tail, Mauby walked away to find a quiet spot.

'But Mauby,' chirped Tiki-Tak, 'you've got to go or Myra's baby will die.'

'Why don't you go, Tiki-Tak?' asked Mauby. 'You can fly there and back in no time.'

'I can't see in the cave. It's too dark. But *cats* can see in the dark. We already figured it out. *You* are the only one who can do it,' said Tiki-Tak.

That evening Mauby went out to the cow pen where Farmer Hunte was tending to the sick calf. She was lying in a corner, breathing heavily. She looked very sick. Mauby wasn't sure what to do. That night she went to sleep very worried.

The next morning Mauby told the other animals that she would go in search of the healing flower.

'Great!' they all shouted, 'but you've got to hurry!'

'There's just one thing,' said Mauby, 'is anyone going to tell me how to get there?'

'You go north till you come to the river. Then you follow the river west up into the mountains,' said Tiki-Tak. 'When you reach the foot of the mountains you will see a waterfall. Right behind the waterfall is a large cave. That's where the healing flower grows.'

Mauby gazed up at the mountains. She wondered what adventures lay in store for her. She tried to hide her fear. She set off across the pasture towards the river.

'Ah . . . there's just one thing,' said Bongo, 'There's a cayman that guards the cave. You'll have to be careful.'

'A cayman,' said Mauby. 'What's that, some stupid long- legged bird?'

'Well, actually, no,' said Tiki-Tak. There was a gleam of mischief in Tiki-Tak's eyes. 'It's a rather large crocodile who eats anything that comes near the cave.'

Mauby stopped in her tracks.

'Nothing to worry about, Mauby. Remember you have *instincts.'* said Bongo. Mauby remembered it was indeed her instincts that had saved her from the macajuel snake in the gully on her last adventure.

Mauby crossed the pasture and slipped through the bougainvillea hedge. She walked beside a field of sweet potatoes and yams.

'Well, well, well!' said a voice from under a tuft of khus khus grass. 'If it isn't my good friend, the cat! And what brings you out here this fine morning?' Sly One, the mongoose, poked his pointed nose out of the grass and fixed his beady eyes on Mauby.

'First of all, you're not my friend. And it's none of your business where I'm going,' said Mauby angrily. She remembered how Sly One had got her into a lot of trouble the last time she had left farm. She kept on walking. Sly One quickly caught up with her, his bushy tail dragging behind him.

'Now, now,' said Sly One, 'remember that it was *I* who taught you to use your instincts. Otherwise you would be dead now.'

Mauby had to admit that Sly One had taught her that in the wild you had to trust your instincts. Perhaps he might be able to help her on this adventure.

'I'm going in search of the magic healing flower that grows in the cave behind the waterfall up in the mountains.'

10

Sly One gave a long whistle. 'Well, that's quite a quest you are on. You'll have to travel up to the mountains. Then you'll have to figure out a way of crossing the river, since the entrance to the cave is on the other bank. And then,' here Sly One paused and stared at the cat, 'you'll have to get by the meanest, most evil creature on God's earth: a huge, horrible cayman with a mouth full of the sharpest, longest teeth you have ever seen. He guards the cave and devours any animal that comes near it. He can swim fast and can run faster and he has a taste for cats.'

Mauby shuddered. What on earth had she got herself into this time? She wondered if it was too late to turn back. Then she remembered that she came from a long line of proud cats. Her cousins in Africa, the lions, would not have been afraid. She would go on and face whatever danger lay in wait for her!

Mauby followed Sly One across several rolling fields until at last they could see the river in the distance. The sun was just beginning to climb in the sky and the sight of the river reminded Mauby how thirsty she was.

'There's a well just over the next rise,' said Sly One. And, as they went over the rise, they could see a well in a field next to a farm. There was a bucket hanging on a rope from the beam over the well.

'There's water in the bucket,' said Sly One, hopping up onto the wall around the well.

'And how do you expect me to get it?' snapped Mauby.

'Easy,' smiled Sly One, 'just watch me.' He leapt onto the beam and scurried along it. He hopped down on to the rim of the bucket and drank some water. Then he climbed back up the rope onto the beam and returned next to Mauby. 'See. Mere child's play.'

But Mauby was far from happy. She was afraid of heights. She peered over the side of the well and saw that it was very deep.

'Look,' said Sly One, 'If you like, I'll hold the rope for you so that it can't slip.' And Sly One gripped in his teeth the rope holding the bucket.

Mauby climbed up onto the beam. She walked along it, trying not to look into the depths of the well. She stretched down to the bucket. Just as her front paws touched the rim, the bucket plunged down into the well.

Mauby screamed and sprang off the bucket. Her front paws narrowly missed the edge of the well. Her claws slid down the

rough stones. She could not get a grip. Just as she thought she would tumble into the black depths, her claws stuck to a vine growing out of the side of the well. She clung to it for dear life.

'Great instincts!' squealed Sly One, peering over the side of the well. 'The vine grows up to the top. You can climb up it.' Then he added, 'Just don't look down. It's a long drop.'

Mauby could have strangled him. But first she had to get out. She gripped the vine tightly with her claws and carefully climbed up to the top. She bounded down to safety on the grass. She turned to face Sly One. Her eyes blazed with fury. She pounced on him and held him to the ground.

'You tried to kill me, didn't you? You were supposed to be holding the rope, you horrid creature!'

'Now, now, now,' said Sly One, trying to wriggle out from underneath Mauby. 'I was holding it, but how was I to know that you were so heavy? It's not my fault; you're too tubby. Ha, ha, a tubby tabby!' Sly One laughed until Mauby tightened her claws on him. 'Okay, okay, I'm sorry! But at least your instincts are working. You jumped out of that bucket real fast.'

Mauby let him go. What was the use? She really shouldn't trust him. She walked off.

'Hey, wait! That's no way to treat a friend. Besides, I know a short cut to the river. All we have to do is pass through this farm.' Sly One pointed to the farm that lay between them and the river.

'Are you sure it's safe?' asked Mauby.

'Safe?!' said Sly One. 'Of course it's safe. I do most of my hunting on that farm. We just have to be cautious, like beasts of the wild, and trust our instincts.'

Mauby shook her head and sighed. She ought to know better, but she was in a hurry to get to the river. She followed Sly One as he slipped under the barbed wire fence that ran along the side of the farm. They went along a ditch and crept close to the farmyard. A few chickens were scratching in the dirt.

19

'Okay,' said Sly One. 'Let's cross the yard.' And without waiting, he shot off across the yard, scattering the chickens. Mauby started to follow when she heard a loud growl, followed by a bark. Looking back, she saw a ferocious pit bull bearing down on her. He was the ugliest dog she had ever seen, and she thought all dogs were ugly. Ahead of her she saw Sly One dart away from the chickens and disappear into a hole in the ground. As she passed the hole, she heard a faint voice hissing, 'Instincts! Use your instincts!'

Mauby had two choices. She could climb a tree or she could try to reach the fence. Without a moment's thought, she dashed for the fence.

She heard the pit bull growling behind her and felt his hot breath on her back. The fence was a few yards ahead of her. She hurled herself through the air, hit the wire and was over the fence just as the dog's jaws closed on her tail, pulling out a tuft of hair.

Mauby didn't stop running until she reached the river. She flopped down at the water's edge, gasping for breath.

'What on earth are you doing here?' A small voice from the river bank startled Mauby. She sprang up and looked around. It was her friend, Clipper, the crab.

'Oh boy, am I ever glad to see you. You wouldn't believe the terrible time I've had!' And Mauby told Clipper all about her quest for the magic healing flower and her adventure with Sly One.

Clipper chuckled. 'I'm sorry to laugh. But I thought you had learned your lesson last time. Never trust that mongoose. He's a trickster. And he has more lives than a cat. Well it looks as if you have quite an adventure ahead of you. It's a long way to the falls. And then you have to cross the river and then . . .' Clipper paused. She looked doubtfully at Mauby. 'Did they tell you about the cayman?'

'Yes,' said Mauby, remembering the danger that lay ahead.

'Well,' said Clipper. 'You'll need all the help you can get, so I'll go with you part of the way and let you meet some of my friends.'

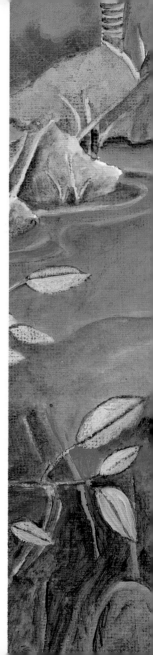

After Mauby had lapped up some cool water, they set off up the river. The bank was lined with coconut and calabash trees. They soon came to a large hole in the ground underneath a tuft of feather grass.

'Ti-lapin!' shouted Clipper. And out of the hole popped a brown hare with the largest ears and widest grin Mauby had ever seen.

'Good to see you, Clipper. What are you doing so far up river?' And he rubbed his paw against Clipper's big claw.

Clipper told him about Mauby's quest. 'I can't go much farther. I want you to go with Mauby to the falls and then see if you can find a way of getting her across the river.'

'Oh, dear, oh dear, oh dear!' said Ti-lapin. 'I would strongly advise you not to go near that waterfall. There is a twenty-foot long cayman with the fiercest set of teeth I've ever seen, and I've only seen them from a great distance.'

Mauby was afraid. But she said she had to go because everyone was depending on her to get the healing flower to stop Myra's baby from dying.

'Well, if you must. But let's get a move on. You need to get there and back before night comes.'

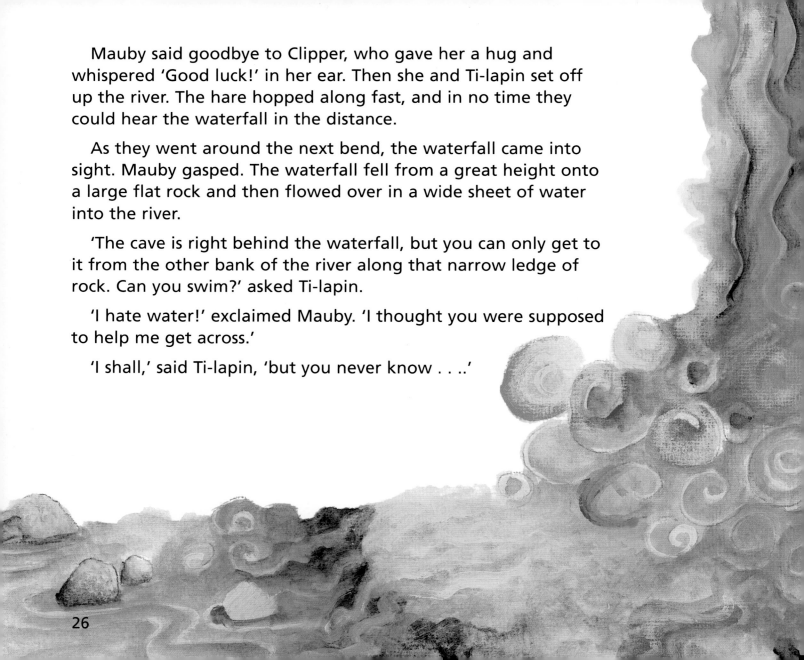

Mauby said goodbye to Clipper, who gave her a hug and whispered 'Good luck!' in her ear. Then she and Ti-lapin set off up the river. The hare hopped along fast, and in no time they could hear the waterfall in the distance.

As they went around the next bend, the waterfall came into sight. Mauby gasped. The waterfall fell from a great height onto a large flat rock and then flowed over in a wide sheet of water into the river.

'The cave is right behind the waterfall, but you can only get to it from the other bank of the river along that narrow ledge of rock. Can you swim?' asked Ti-lapin.

'I hate water!' exclaimed Mauby. 'I thought you were supposed to help me get across.'

'I shall,' said Ti-lapin, 'but you never know . . ..'

Ti-lapin looked up into the overhanging mango tree and gave a loud whistle. A burst of chattering came from above. A monkey swung down from the tree and landed right in front of them. 'How's tricks, my brother Ti-lapin?' the monkey said, tapping the hare with his paw.

'Fine, just fine, Makak. I want you to meet our sister Mauby from down in the foot hills. She wants to cross the river.' Ti-lapin paused. 'She is on a quest for the magic healing flower from the cave.'

There was a loud chorus of shrieks from above. Looking up, Mauby saw a troop of monkeys peering down at them from the lower branches of the tree.

'I would gladly take you across the river, my dear,' said Makak to Mauby, 'but I would be taking you to your death. No one has ever come out of that cave alive, except Ligaru, the cayman.'

'Tell her about Ligaru, Makak, and maybe she will turn back.' At this all the other monkeys slid down to the ground and gathered around Makak, tucking their tails beneath them.

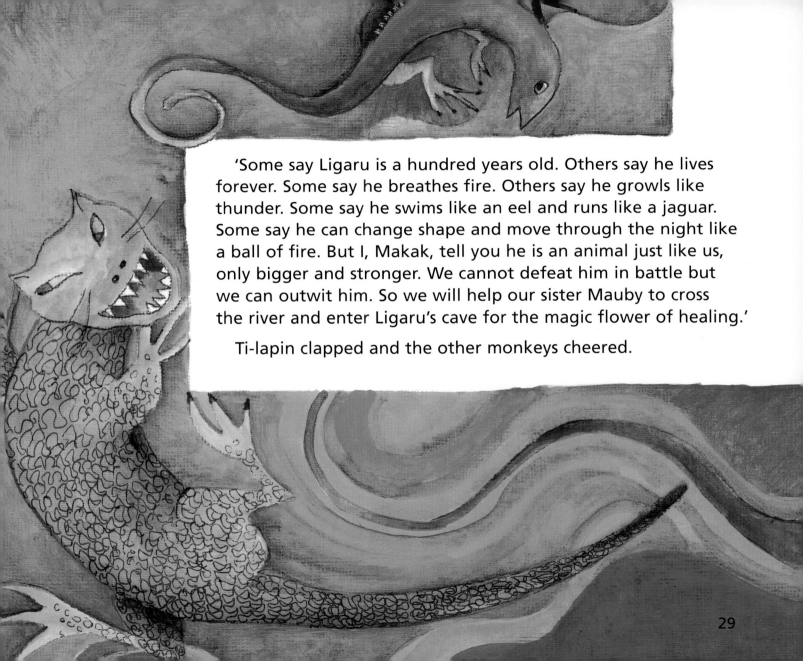

'Some say Ligaru is a hundred years old. Others say he lives forever. Some say he breathes fire. Others say he growls like thunder. Some say he swims like an eel and runs like a jaguar. Some say he can change shape and move through the night like a ball of fire. But I, Makak, tell you he is an animal just like us, only bigger and stronger. We cannot defeat him in battle but we can outwit him. So we will help our sister Mauby to cross the river and enter Ligaru's cave for the magic flower of healing.'

Ti-lapin clapped and the other monkeys cheered.

'Let us not waste any more time in idle chatter. We have work to do.' And grabbing Mauby with one hand, Makak swung up into the mango tree. He flew from branch to branch and then hurled himself into the air across the river and just managed to grab a branch of the banyan tree on the opposite bank. The branch bent under their weight and they skimmed the surface of the water. Mauby, who had kept her eyes tightly closed, thought they were falling into the river. But Makak, using his free hand, climbed quickly up the tree and then down onto the bank.

Mauby breathed a great sigh of relief.

'Now, listen to me carefully,' said Makak. 'We are going to lure Ligaru out of the cave. While we are doing that, you go along the ledge by the waterfall and go into the cave. Pick the magic flower and get out of there fast. Run along the bank till you reach this tree. Climb up it and wait for me.'

'How are you going to get Ligaru out of the cave?' asked Mauby.

'You'll see. Now run along and hide behind that bush next to the ledge and as soon as you see Ligaru come out of the cave, you go!'

Mauby crept up to the bush next to the ledge. Her heart was beating so loud she thought Ligaru was sure to hear it. As she slipped behind the bush, she saw Makak and five other monkeys dangling with tails and arms linked from a branch overhanging the river. The last monkey was touching the water. They all started to scream loudly and the monkey at the bottom of the chain beat the water with his hands.

Mauby heard a sound which made her hair stand on end. It was a deep, low growl like distant thunder. It came from behind the waterfall. She saw a large green snout appear; then two red eyes. The cayman stopped and looked at the river. It saw the monkeys. It opened its mouth full of long yellow teeth and, with a big roar, dived into the river and sank beneath the water.

Mauby stood still, unable to move. Then she heard Makak's voice: 'Now, Mauby, now!' Mauby crept along the narrow ledge hugging the face of the cliff. She did not look down but kept her eyes on the entrance to the cave. She darted inside the cave. It was damp and dark. It smelt horrible.

She waited while her eyes got accustomed to the dark. She saw something white glimmering on the walls of the cave. She went closer and saw that they were tiny white flowers growing on a vine. This must be the magic healing flower. She climbed up the wall. She reached out with her paw and tore off a bunch of the flowers. They smelt sweet.

Mauby picked up the flowers in her mouth and ran back to
the entrance of the cave. She poked her head out and was
amazed by what she saw. Makak and his troop of monkeys were
still hanging from the branch, but now about three feet above
the water. Suddenly, the surface of the water was broken by the
enormous head of the cayman. It lunged upwards, and snapped
its jaws, barely missing the lowest monkey. They all shrieked.

Mauby's mouth fell open in astonishment. The flowers dropped
out and landed on the brink of the ledge. Mauby's paw shot out.
Too late. The wind blew the flowers off the ledge into the water
below. Mauby leaned over and tried to reach the flowers with
one paw.

'Watch out, Mauby!' she heard Makak shout. She looked up
and saw that Ligaru had turned around and was now heading
her way. His red eyes gleamed wickedly.

At that moment, Mauby lost her grip and fell into the river.
She sank beneath the swirling water. She came up spluttering.
She grasped the bunch of magic flowers in her mouth. The force
of the water carried her towards the bank of the river. But not
fast enough. She could see Ligaru bearing down on her. His long
tail thrashed the water. She paddled furiously. She was still about
six feet from the bank.

Just as she was giving up hope, Makak appeared on the bank and held out the branch of a coconut tree to her. Mauby crawled up the branch and bounded to safety. She could hear the loud crunch as the crocodile's jaws tore into the branch.

Mauby and the monkey dashed for the nearest tree. Ligaru was hot on their heels. She had no idea a cayman could run that fast. She heard a loud roar right behind her. Mauby and Makak reached the tree at the same time. They scrambled up its trunk and didn't stop until they were perched on the highest branch.

Mauby gasped and the magic healing flowers fell out of her mouth. Makak caught them just in time.

'Careful,' said Makak, as he handed them back to Mauby. 'Well, I'm sure now that cats have nine lives. But you are also a very brave cat.'

'It is you who are brave, Makak,' said Mauby. 'Without your help, I would never have got these healing flowers. But I must go now if I am to get back before dark. The sun will set in about two hours' time and I really don't want to spend another night in a tree.' Mauby was thinking of her night in the gully with the macajuel snake.

Makak and his troop soon took Mauby safely across the river. She said goodbye to the monkeys and Ti-lapin and began her journey home. She carried the healing flowers firmly in her mouth. She met Clipper on her way and said goodbye. She avoided the farm with the pit bull and did not see Sly One at all.

When she reached the outskirts of her own farm, night was beginning to fall. She ran into the farm yard. All the animals were gathered around the pen where Myra's calf lay sick. Bongo saw her and started to bark furiously.

Tiki-tak flew to meet her.

'You did it! You did it!' cried Tiki-tak excitedly. She looked carefully at the flowers that Mauby was carrying in her mouth. 'And they are the right ones. Good for you, Mauby!'

As Mauby came up to the cow pen, Bongo barked furiously and pulled at Farmer Hunte's hand.

'What's the matter, Bongo?' said Farmer Hunte, who had been talking to the vet.

Mauby placed the healing flowers at Farmer Hunte's feet. He bent down and picked them up. The vet looked at them closely and sniffed them. 'Well I'll be ... !' he said yes. 'These are the flowers of the cave vine. The old folk used to give them to sheep and cattle as a medicine. I haven't seen these for a long time. Well, there's no harm in trying, since my medicine isn't working.'

The vet plucked some flowers from the cluster. He leant over and put them in the calf's mouth. She chewed them slowly. After a long while, the calf raised her head and gave a little moo. Everybody cheered. She would live.

Later that night, Mauby told her adventures to Myra, Bongo and Tiki-tak. Then she drank a warm bowl of milk and settled down to a nice night's sleep.

As she drifted off to sleep, she kept on repeating, 'Never will I leave the farm again. Never will I leave the farm . . .'

47

Macmillan Education
Between Towns Road, Oxford OX4 3PP
A division of Macmillan Publishers Limited
Companies and representatives throughout the world

www.macmillan-caribbean.com

ISBN 0 333 95313 4

Text © Peter Laurie 2001
Design and illustration © Macmillan Publishers Limited 2001

First published 2001

Designed by Alex Tucker, Holbrook Design Oxford Limited
Illustrated by H. Ann Dodson

Printed in China

2005 2004 2003 2002 2001
10 9 8 7 6 5 4 3 2 1